Wiggle and the Whale
a book of funny friends

Roger Priddy

priddy books

For best friends everywhere

Illustrated by Lindsey Sagar
Based on original illustrations by Jo Ryan

This book was made by Mara van der Meer,
Penny Worms, Hannah Cockayne, and Kate Ward.

Copyright © 2016 St. Martin's Press, LLC
175 Fifth Avenue, New York, NY 10010
Created for St. Martin's Press by priddy✿books

1 3 5 7 9 10 8 6 4 2
Manufactured in China March 2016

Picture credits: Ice skate © Amorphis / iStock Photo; Macaroons © Emmanuelle Guillou / Alamy;
Pink cotton candy © DarrenMower / iStock Photo; Pencil © Sezeryadigar / iStock Photo;
Pink feather boa © Superstock / Alamy; Pine cone © ivstiv / iStock Photo;
Ice cubes © ryasick / iStock Photo; Sequins © kilukilu / iStock Photo;
Diamond © royaltystockphoto / iStock Photo.

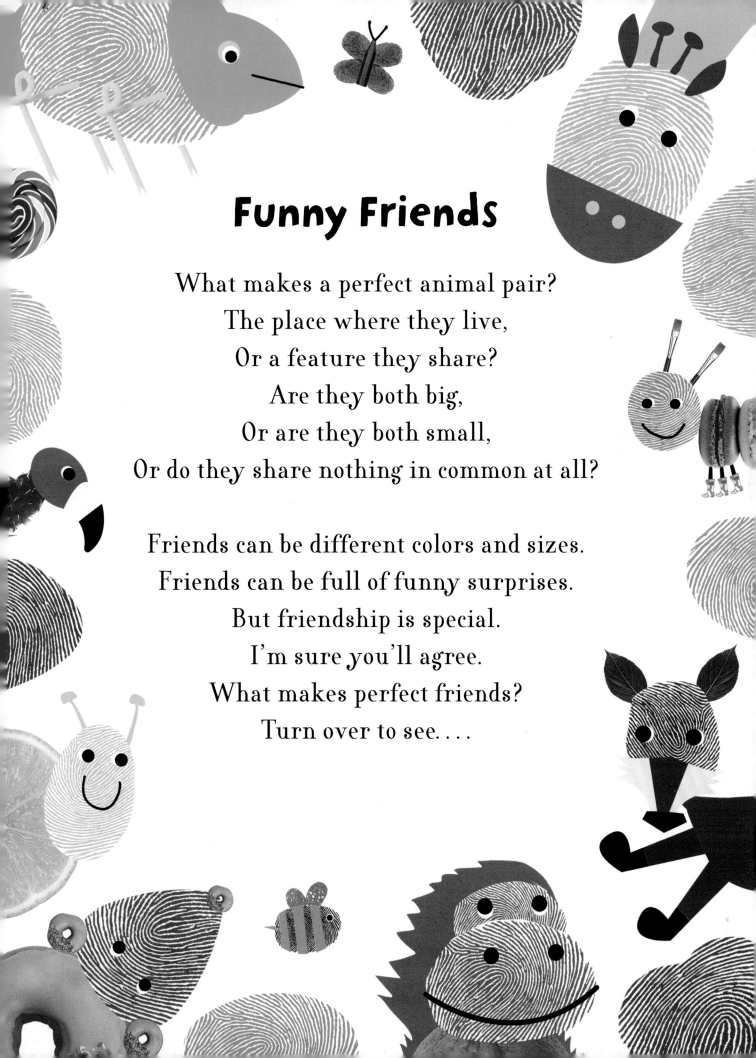

Funny Friends

What makes a perfect animal pair?
The place where they live,
Or a feature they share?
Are they both big,
Or are they both small,
Or do they share nothing in common at all?

Friends can be different colors and sizes.
Friends can be full of funny surprises.
But friendship is special.
I'm sure you'll agree.
What makes perfect friends?
Turn over to see. . . .

Jellyfish

I am a jolly jellyfish.
I wiggle in the sea.
No other fish can wiggle
Just as perfectly as me.

Blue Whale

I'm big and blue and brainy.
I travel far and wide,
But I'm never quite as happy
As when Wiggle's by my side.

Crocodile

I'm very pleased to meet you.
I'm King Louis of the Swamp.
My feet go waddle, waddle,
And my teeth go chomp, chomp, chomp!

Chameleon

King Louis is my reptile friend.
We're as different as can be.
And when he's very hungry,
I like hiding in a tree.

Lion

Hello, lion fans! I'm Leo the Great.
A lion with a fearsome roar.
I might be vain,
But look at my mane!
I'm a cat you just can't ignore.

Zebra

Little Zena the zebra
Is stripy and so shy,
But her heart goes
BOOM! BOOM! BOOM!
Whenever Leo struts by.

Walrus

I'm Walter the walrus.
I like lounging on the shore.
I have two long tusks and a very loud roar.
On the ice, I like lazing.
In the water, I'm amazing!
Just like Penguin, I can swim and glide and soar.

Penguin

I am a little penguin.
See me slide across the ice.
Walter might look scary,
But he's really very nice!

Hippopotamus

Isn't it preposterous
How big old gray rhinoceros
Has funny horns upon his head?
Hippos are shorter.
We wallow in the water,
So we have massive nostrils instead.

Rhinoceros

I am Grumpy Rhinoceros.
He's Happy Hippopotamus.
We're different beyond any doubt.
He laughs. I growl.
He smiles. I scowl.
But we both like stomping about.

Giraffe

No animal is taller.
I'm the tallest of them all!
I have a friend called Caterpillar.
He's teeny-tiny small.

Fox

I am Lox the fox.
I walk the forest trail.
I have soft, red fur,
And a very bushy tail.

Caterpillar

I'm a wriggly little creature,
Always ready for a laugh.
But no-one's so hilarious
As silly old Giraffe!

Squirrel

I am Cyril the squirrel.
My tail is bushy too.
With Lox, I dance the fox-trot
At the Woodland Boogaloo!

Toucan

I'm Lucan the toucan, a bird with a beak
Over twice the size of my head!
When feeding, it's useful,
But if I'm being truthful
I'd rather have sharp teeth instead.

Iguana

My name is Alana.
I'm a little green iguana.
I can climb to the top of any tree,
Where I can watch Lucan,
A majestic toucan,
Soaring in the sky above me.

Orangutan

Look at me! Up in the tree!
I'm the star of the show!
I'm gymnastic!
Look fantastic!
As I'm swinging to and fro!

Flamingo

Hola, mi amigo!
I'm Fifi the flamingo.
I have charm and a dazzling smile.
My feathers are pink
From the water I drink.
I'm a bird with unquestionable style.

Horse

I'm Henry the horse,
I'm fast, of course.
My friend is a snail called Slow.
As odd as we seem,
We make a great team.
She's the brains,
I'm the get-up-and-go!

Snail

Hello! Hello! My name is Slow.
Without any feet, I need slime to go.
But being with Henry is such a blast.
I get on his back and we go really fast!

Bear

Don't you know, it's rude to stare?
Have you never seen a pink baby bear?
My name is Bo,
And I don't like snow,
So I'm off to my cozy lair.

Hedgehog

I'm Snuffles the hedgehog.
A sharp and prickly thing.
I love to hibernate with Bo.
I'll see you next spring!

Best Friends

Best of friends, you've met them all.
Wriggly, giggly, big, and small.
Friends, they care. Friends are fun.
And that's the end. Our book is done.